THIS IS IT

BY DARIA PEOPLES-RILEY

Greenwillow Books, *An Imprint of* HarperCollins*Publishers*

For Jonah Marie
*The Lord your God will be with you
wherever you go.*

This Is It. Copyright © 2018 by Daria Peoples-Riley. All rights reserved. Printed in China. For information address HarperCollins Children's Books, a division of HarperCollins Publishers, 195 Broadway, New York, NY 10007. www.harpercollinschildrens.com
This art was painted with black sumi ink, gouache, and watercolor on paper, and then digitally composited in Photoshop. The text type is Kandal Book.
Library of Congress Cataloging-in-Publication Data is available. ISBN 978-0-06-265776-3 (trade ed.)
22 SCP 10 9   First Edition   Greenwillow Books

Look at me.

Stand

up

tall.

Arch your back.

Hold

your

head

high.

You've been dancing since you came to be.

Little bun and rosy cheeks.
Little hands and fat flat feet.

Up and up,
      down and down.

           Tapping toes
                on concrete street—
                    DANCING!

The future is in your footsteps.
Freedom is in your feet.
Put one in front of the other,
and greet your destiny.

Shhh. . . .

Listen to the hum of your heart's song.
It will never lead you wrong.

Dance with all your might.

Grace flows
from your soul
to your fingertips.

Rhythms beat
 all
  the
   way
    down
     your spine.

Stand up tall.
Arch your back.
Hold your head high.